LITTLE MONSTER'S BEDTIME BOOK

by Mercer Mayer

to
Kathleen

MERRIGOLD PRESS • NEW YORK

When it's time to sleep,
Pop reads to me.

Tonight he is reading monster rhymes.

THE KERPLOPPUS

Your favorite monster has bright blue ears,
And scales from purple to yellow.
By day he gobbles up dirt and stones,
By night he's a cozy bedfellow.

THE GRITHIX

When Humpty Dumpty fell off the wall,
The Grithix couldn't fix him at all.
The Grithix got grumpy, but Humpty felt worse,
So they went off together to find him a nurse.

THE QUANDREY

The Quandrey's always in a knot.
You see, he changes his mind a lot.
Back or forth, to or fro,
He can never decide which way to go.

THE STAMP-COLLECTING TROLLUSK

A book filled with stamps is the Trollusk's delight.
He spends happy hours both day and night,
Looking through pages admiring the design
Of stamps that he's stolen from your mail
   and mine.

THE YALAPAPPUS

Oh, Yalapappus, you silly beast,
You think that paper is a feast.
Yesterday's news is your favorite lunch,
And you serve paper bags when friends
   come for brunch.

THE JURFUS

If under the ground you should
    happen to go,
You might meet the Jurfus—
    he lives down below.
His lair's cold and danky,
And he tends to be cranky,
So watch out lest he nibble your toe.

THE WHIZZLE

The Whizzle heaves a helpless sigh,
For he is far too fat to fly.
He forgets his size is his
   own fault,
So he drinks another malt.

THE CROONIE

There are many strange
  creatures living in trees,
And the strangest I know
  has large, knobby knees.
If, while you are dreaming,
  a Croonie you meet,
You'll notice she wears granny
  shoes on her feet.

THE PEEVISH

If the Peevish loses, he just won't play.
He takes his marbles and grumps away.
With a great big frown he sulks in his cave.
Are you like a Peevish? Or do you behave?

THE TYPHOONIGATOR

The Typhoonigator is a windy beast.
He huffs and puffs from West to East.
And when there's nothing left to say,
He simply blows himself away.

THE HEFALO

The Hefalo's a hefty fellow.
If hurt he gives a hefty bellow.
So be careful when you're flying by;
Don't poke the Hefalo in the eye.

THE BLOWFAT-GLOWFISH

The Blowfat-Glowfish
Likes to play "Go Fish."
He has a little light,
So he can play at night.

THE BABY GREAT GLERN OF THE SEA

The Baby Great Glern of the Sea
Gives annoying advice constantly.
"Now if that hand were mine,
I'd throw the nine.
My goodness, you'd lose
   without me!"

THE GRUMLEY

The Grumley will help
If you're stranded at sea.
He'll tow you to shore,
And safe you will be.

THE USELESS

At last you're ready to be
  on your way,
But the silly Useless wants
  you to stay.
He throws up his hands and
  lets out a moan.
Don't you wish the Useless
  would leave you alone?

Stories have beginnings and stories have ends,
So say goodbye to all your friends.
And now that we've finished the very last rhyme,
We'll close the book until the next time.

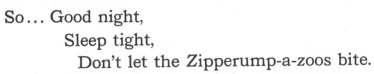

So... Good night,
Sleep tight,
Don't let the Zipperump-a-zoos bite.